For Marvel, Oleson, and Rye.
—H.M.

For my nieces.
—S.G.

The Stocking Stuffer

For information address HarperCollins Children's Books, a division of HarperCollins Publishers, 195 Broadway, New York, NY 10007.
www.harpercollinschildrens.com

Library of Congress Control Number: 2021945754
ISBN 978-0-06-314207-7

The artist used Adobe Fresco and Adobe Photoshop to create the digital illustrations for this book.
Typography by Honee Jang
Hand Lettering by Alexis Snell
22 23 24 25 26 RTLO 10 9 8 7 6 5 4 3 2 1
❖
First Edition

The Stocking Stuffer

Written by
Holley Merriweather

Illustrated by
Stephanie Graegin

HARPER
An Imprint of HarperCollins*Publishers*

'Twas the night before Christmas, when not long ago,
A tradition began that few children know.
A blizzard was raging up at the North Pole,
Elves rushed as the winds howled out of control.

"Are we ready?" called Santa. "There's no time to waste.
It's the worst Christmas storm that we've ever faced."
"Almost," said an elf as she slid on the ice.
"But are you sure that you've checked the list twice?"

Taking the scroll from the elf's shaking grasp,
Santa put on his glasses and said with a gasp—
"The Naughty List is empty! This is a first.
What a glorious Christmas—I feel I could burst!"

"It's a miracle," she said, "for all to enjoy.
But I must tell the elves that we need some more toys!
With all of the children now on the Nice List,
We need to make sure that no one is missed."

"Please hurry, little one, the storm's getting stronger.
With so much to do, we can't wait too much longer.
I'll need some help from every last elf.
How else will I finish Christmas Eve by myself?"

The elf left the barn with a nod and a hop
To finish the toys in Santa's workshop.
Santa took a deep breath and reached for his cup.
He needed some cocoa to help him perk up!

What Santa didn't know was that I had been listening,
Hidden under the tree with the Christmas lights glistening.
I loved watching Saint Nick, the elves, and reindeer
As they made and wrapped presents
throughout the whole year.

I'd wanted a job, like an elf on a shelf,
But I had no magic, just my little mouse self.
If every child was on the Nice List,
There'd be no time for stockings. I'd have to assist!
This was my moment, my dream could come true.
Santa would see I'd be great on his crew.

I'm Tinsel the mouse. I live under the tree.
Curled up by the presents is where you'll find me.
But this year I'm ready to join on the sleigh
And bring goodies and gifts for a warm Christmas Day.
While you're busy unpacking your bag full of treats
I could fill stockings with trinkets and sweets."

Santa crinkled his brow and scratched at his beard.
Was he not happy that I'd volunteered?

Then his eyes lit up bright and his fingers snapped quick.
"Tinsel, my friend, will you join Old Saint Nick?"
I clapped my paws and twirled on my toe.
"I'll help you, Santa. I'm ready to go!"

The elves finished wrapping and loading the treats
As Santa and I snuggled into our seats.
"On, Dancer! On, Prancer! On, Vixen! On, Comet!
We're running late now. It's time to step on it!"

Rudolph's red nose lit up with a glow
As the sleigh took flight straight out of the snow.
We waved a goodbye to our wintry North Pole
And set our sights south with not one lump of coal.

Santa jiggled and wiggled into the first flue.

It was finally time! We had a big job to do!

I leaped and tumbled from Santa's red cap,
Straightened my collar and fixed my bootstrap.

Santa hefted his bag from the hearth to the tree,
Unpacking and stacking the presents with glee.
"A drum set for Dad, a skateboard for Ike,
For Mom, an easel, for Dottie, a bike.
A squeak toy for Pepper . . ." the family's new pug,
Who sat and watched Santa from her place on the rug.

I spotted the stockings hanging high in a row.
I set down my bag and undid the bow.
This was my chance, my first Christmas Eve,
To help bring good cheer to those who believe.

"Dad gets gumdrops and brand-new drumsticks.
For Mom, paintbrushes and licorice whips.
For Dottie, a puzzle and a sweet candy cane.
Ike gets a lollipop and a model airplane.
And finally, Pepper gets a tasty new bone.
We're all done here, Santa, on to the next home!"

Ike
Dottie

"Not yet, Tinsel, there's still more to do.
We've got to fuel up to see this night through!
It's time to share treats from Ike and from Dottie.
They made them to show us they're nice and not naughty."

We ate up the cookies—"Tiny Tin, have one more!"
I nibbled so fast that some fell to the floor.

A swift and small creature made a mad dash,
Scooped up some crumbs and was gone in a flash.

"What was that?" whispered Santa. "Did you just see?"

"Oh, yes!" I exclaimed. "'Twas a mouse, just like *me*."

I thought I was done, but it wasn't enough.

It turned out I had one more stocking to stuff.

I took off my sock and hung it up high,
And filled it with gifts for the *mouse* who ran by.

As we rallied the reindeer to leave the warm house,
I called down the chimney, "Sweet dreams, little mouse."

We went on to visit each girl and each boy,
Delivering presents and spreading true joy!
As we trotted the globe, making our way,
No one was forgotten on this holiday.

I stuffed every stocking on mantels galore,
And when something was missing, I left a bit more.
At the last house, I cheered with my friend,
"Hooray, the Naughty List comes to an end!"

As Christmas Eve quietly came to a close,
I nestled on top of Rudolph's red nose.
Santa called out and sang with a grin,
"Merry Christmas to *all*, thanks to you, Tiny Tin."

So don't you forget in your letter this year,
It's Santa *and* Tinsel who bring Christmas cheer.
Write down your wishes, and send them on through,
To Old Saint Nick and the Stocking Stuffer, too.

FOREVER
SANTA and TINSEL
the North POLE